My "r" Sound Box®

(Blends are included in this book.)

Library of Congress Cataloging-in-Publication Data
Moncure, Jane Belk.
My "r" sound box / by Jane Belk Moncure.
p. cm.
Summary: A little boy fills his sound box with many words that begin with the letter "r."
ISBN 1-56766-784-8
[1. Alphabet.] I. Title.
PZ7.M739 Myr   2000
[E]—dc21   99-054325

My "r" Sound Box®

Jane Belk Moncure

illustrated by Colin King

The Child's World®

Little  had a box.

"I will find things that begin with my 'r' sound," he said. "I will put them into my sound box."

Little  found rabbits

and radishes.

Did he put the rabbits and radishes into the box? He did.

Little  found a rooster.

Did he put the rooster into the box with the rabbits and radishes? He did.

Then he found a raccoon.

The raccoon ran!

Little  ran after the raccoon . . .

and put him into the box.

Then he saw a rat.

The rat ran.

Little  ran after the rat

and put him into the box.

Then he ran down the road.

Soon Little  r met a reindeer.

The reindeer was too big for the box, so Little r found a

rowboat.

He put the reindeer and the box with
the rat, the raccoon, the rooster, and
the rabbits   into the rowboat.

There were no radishes left.
The rabbits had eaten the radishes.

Little rowed down the river.

But it rained.

Little put on his raincoat.

He rowed right into a . . .

rhinoceros.

The rhinoceros was too big

for the rowboat.

So Little r found a

raft.

He put all the animals on the raft.
He put the box on the raft, too.

But the raft ran into a rock.

The reindeer, the rat, and the rooster

fell off the raft.

Little  found

a rope . . .

and rescued them!

"Now we will rest!" he said.

The rhinoceros, the rabbits, the raccoon, the reindeer, the rat, and the rooster rested . . .

under a
rainbow.

Little   rested, too.

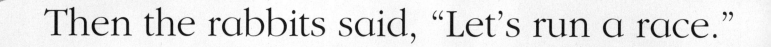

Then the rabbits said, "Let's run a race."

They ran up the road to . . .

a bush full of 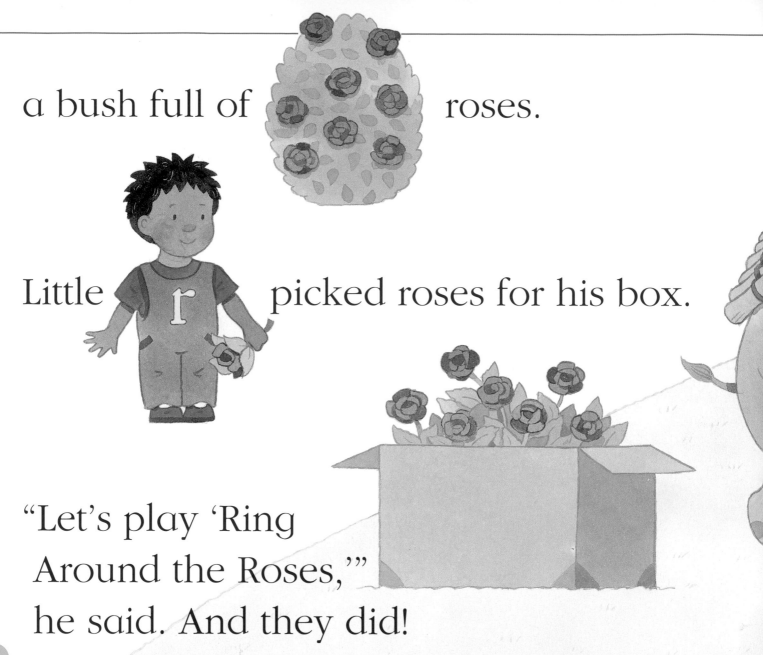 roses.

Little picked roses for his box.

"Let's play 'Ring Around the Roses,'" he said. And they did!

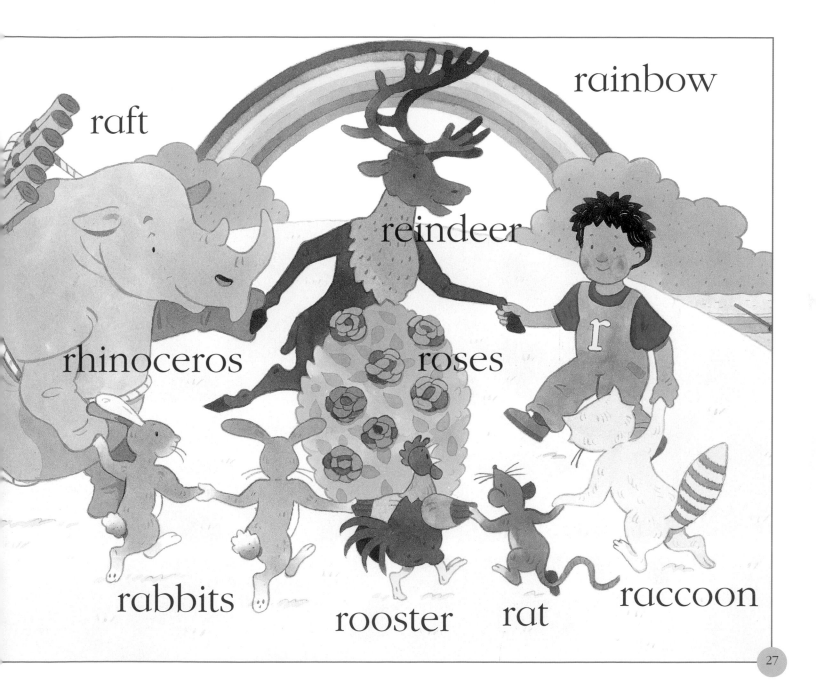

raft

rainbow

reindeer

rhinoceros

roses

rabbits

rooster

rat

raccoon

Can you read these words with Little r ?

razor

robe

robin

red

rattlesnake

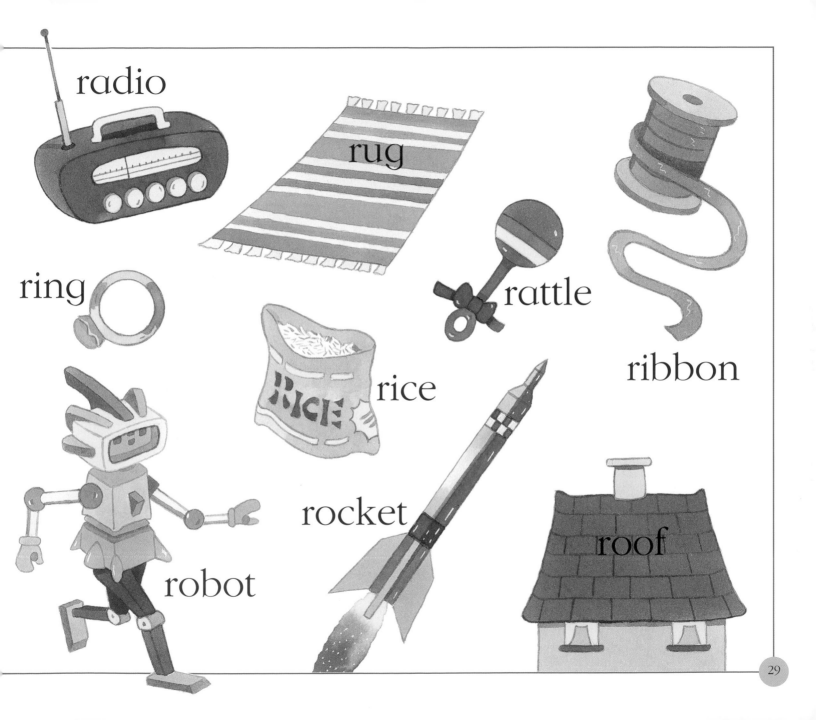

radio

rug

ring

rattle

ribbon

rice

robot

rocket

roof

ABOUT THE AUTHOR AND ILLUSTRATOR

Jane Belk Moncure began her writing career when she was in kindergarten. She has never stopped writing. Many of her children's stories and poems have been published, to the delight of young readers, including her son Jim, whose childhood experiences found their way into many of her books.

Mrs. Moncure's writing is based upon an active career in early childhood education. A recipient of an M.A. degree from Columbia University, Mrs. Moncure has taught and directed nursery, kindergarten, and primary grade programs in California, New York, Virginia, and North Carolina. As a former member of the faculties of Virginia Commonwealth University and the University of Richmond, she taught prospective teachers in early childhood education.

Mrs. Moncure has travelled extensively abroad, studying early childhood programs in the United Kingdom, The Netherlands, and Switzerland. She was the first president of the Virginia Association for Early Childhood Education and received its award for outstanding service to young children.

A resident of North Carolina, Mrs. Moncure is currently a full-time writer and educational consultant. She is married to Dr. James A. Moncure, former vice president of Elon College.

Colin King studied at the Royal College of Art, London. He started his freelance career as an illustrator, working for magazines and advertising agencies.

He began drawing pictures for children's books in 1976 and has illustrated over sixty titles to date.

Included in a wide variety of subjects are a best-selling children's encyclopedia and books about spies and detectives.

His books have been translated into several languages, including Japanese and Hebrew. He has four grown-up children and lives in Suffolk, England, with his wife, three dogs, and a cat.